Santa's Big Day

Another year has come and gone
I've counted every day.
And now it's finally Christmas Eve–
I must be on my way!

The toys and games are ready now,
The sled waits in the snow.
The reindeer prance impatiently–
It's their big night, you know!

Where are my gloves? My boots? My hat?
It's time to be away!
And let's wish people everywhere
A Merry Christmas Day!

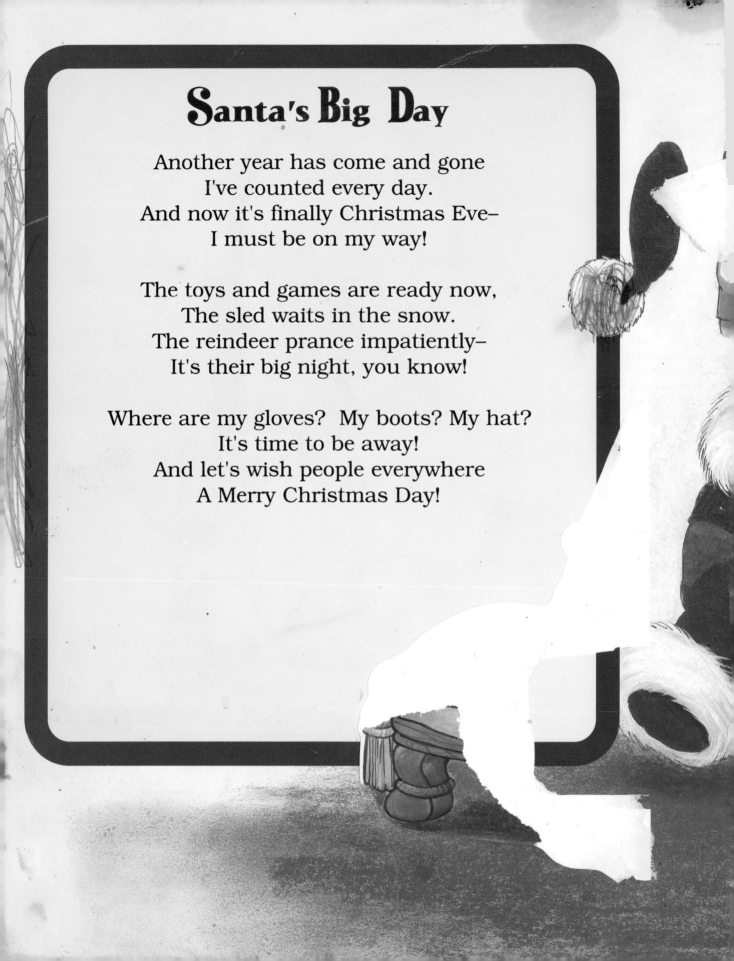

 "A Visit from St. Nicholas"

by Clement Clarke Moore

"Now, Dasher! now, Dancer!
now, Prancer and Vixen!
On Comet! on, Cupid!
on, Donder and Blitzen!

To the top of the porch!
to the top of the wall!
Now dash away! dash away!
Dash away, all!"

He sprang to his sleigh,
to his team gave a whistle,
And away they all flew
like the down of a thistle.

But I heard him exclaim,
ere he drove out of sight,
"Happy Christmas to all,
and to all a good night!"

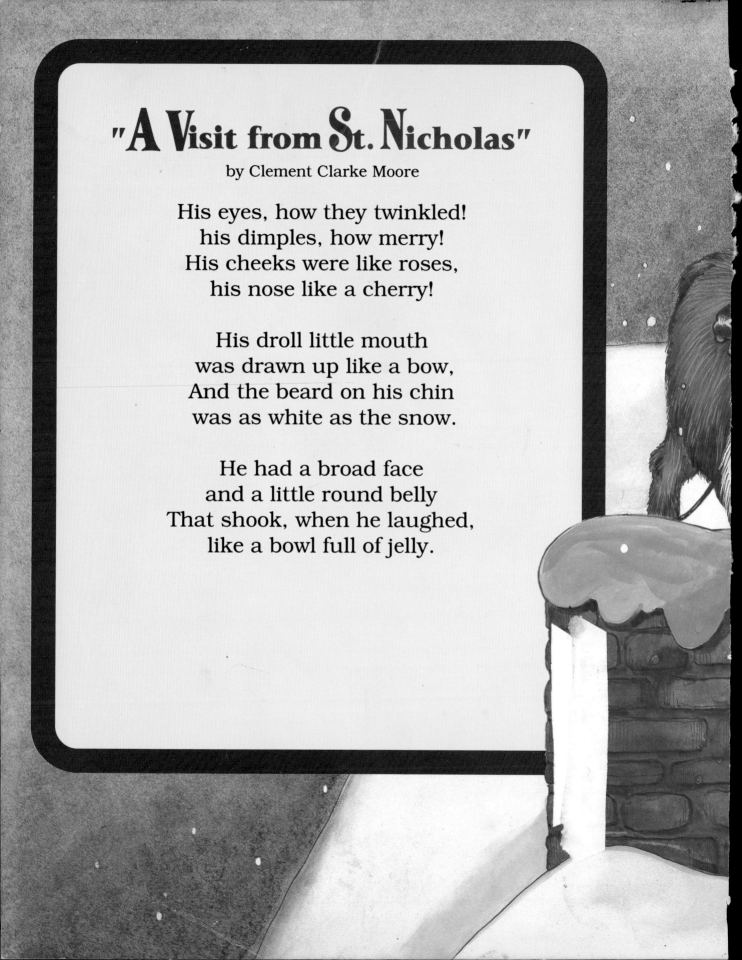

"A Visit from St. Nicholas"

by Clement Clarke Moore

His eyes, how they twinkled!
his dimples, how merry!
His cheeks were like roses,
his nose like a cherry!

His droll little mouth
was drawn up like a bow,
And the beard on his chin
was as white as the snow.

He had a broad face
and a little round belly
That shook, when he laughed,
like a bowl full of jelly.

A Christmas Surprise

What a delight!
What a surprise!
To find Santa napping
before our own eyes!

He must have been tired
from dropping off toys
To homes round the world
for all good girls and boys.

Now here he is, sleeping
in Daddy's big chair!
While we tiptoe closer
to whisper and stare.

Do you dare to wake him?
Oh no, dear, not I!
We'll just sit and watch him,
for we're all too shy.

Let's creep back to bed now,
for I'm sleepy, too.
And if I've just dreamed this,
Did you
dream it too?